Rapunzel

by BERNICE CHARDIET

Pictures by KRISTINA RODANAS

SCHOLASTIC BOOK SERVICES
NEW YORK • TORONTO • LONDON • AUCKLAND • SYDNEY • TOKYO

ISBN 0-590-30960-9

Text copyright © 1982 by Bernice Chardiet. Illustrations copyright © 1982 by Kristina Rodanas. Published by Scholastic Book Services, a division of Scholastic Inc.

12 11 10 9 8 7 6 5 4 3 2 1   1   2 3 4 5 6/8
Printed in the U.S.A.

18

For my mother,
Florence Kroll Raybin

Once upon a time a man and his wife
lived next door to a powerful witch.

The witch had a beautiful garden.
There was a high wall all around it.
No one ever went there.

But the wife could see over the wall
from her window upstairs.

One day she saw some new green plants
growing in the witch's garden.
They were tender radish plants, called rapunzels.
As soon as she saw them,
the wife wanted to eat them.
She wanted them so much,
she would not eat anything else.

She grew thinner and thinner
until her husband said,
"Dear wife, what is wrong with you?"

"Oh, husband," said the wife,
"I want some rapunzels.
I want some rapunzels from the witch's garden.
If I do not get some rapunzels to eat,
I will die!"

So that night, the husband climbed
over the garden wall.
He grabbed a handful of rapunzels
and took them home to his wife.

The wife ate the rapunzels at once.
The next day she wanted more.
She wanted them twice as much as before.

"Oh, husband," she cried.
"You must get me more rapunzels.
If you do not get them, I know I will die."

The husband waited until it was dark.
Then he climbed the wall again.

But this time, the witch
was in the garden.
"Thief!" she shouted. "So you're the one!
You're the one who steals my rapunzels!"

"Oh, please!" the man said.
"Do not be angry.
Let me have some rapunzels.
My wife will die without them."

"Well, then," said the witch.
"Take all the rapunzels you want."

"Oh, thank you!" the man said.

"But," said the witch,
"you must give me something for them."

"I will give you anything you say,"
the man promised.

"Soon your wife will have a child,"
the witch said.
"You must give that child to me!
If you do not, your wife must die."

What could the poor man do?
He took the rapunzels,
and sadly he went home.

A few months later,
the wife had a baby girl.
The witch came at once.
She named the baby Rapunzel
and took her away.

Each year, Rapunzel
grew more and more beautiful.
By the time she was twelve years old,
she was the most beautiful child
in the world.

Her golden hair shone like the sun.
It was so long
it trailed on the ground
and made a golden path behind her.

On Rapunzel's twelfth birthday,
the witch took her deep into the forest
and shut her away in a tower.

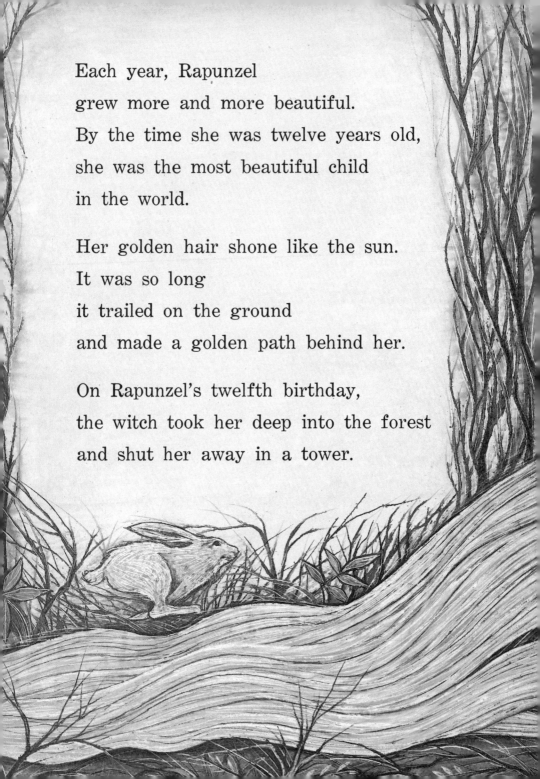

There were no stairs in the tower.
There was not even a door.
There was only a window
way up at the top.

Every day, the witch
would come to the tower and call,
  Rapunzel, Rapunzel!
  Let down your hair!

Then Rapunzel would unpin
her long, long braids
and let them down from the window.
The witch would grab the ends and climb up.

For years, Rapunzel saw no one but the witch.
Then, one day a prince came riding
through the forest.
He heard someone singing
and stopped to listen.
It was Rapunzel, singing in the tower.

Her song was so lovely,
the prince followed the sound.
He came to the tower,
but he could not get inside.

The prince went away.
But he came back every day
to listen to Rapunzel singing.

One morning, he saw the witch coming.
He hid behind a tree
and heard the witch call,
  Rapunzel, Rapunzel!
  Let down your hair!

Then long, golden braids
came down from the window
and the witch climbed up.

"So that's the way it's done,"
thought the prince.
"Well, I will climb the golden ladder too."

The prince waited until the witch left.
It was almost dark.
Then he ran to the tower and called,
  Rapunzel, Rapunzel!
  Let down your hair!

In a moment, the golden braids
came down from the window.
Quickly the prince climbed up.

Rapunzel was frightened.
But he spoke to her so softly,
she began to lose her fear.
She could see how young and handsome he was
— not at all like the witch.
She agreed to go away with him
and be his wife.

But how could she get out of the tower?

"We must make a ladder,"
she said to the prince.
"Every time you come,
bring me strong silk thread.
I will weave the thread into a ladder.
When the ladder is finished,
we will go away together."

So every night the prince came,
and Rapunzel worked on the ladder.
And every day the witch came,
and Rapunzel hid the ladder away.

One day, without thinking,
Rapunzel said to the witch,
"Why does it take you so long to climb up?
You are so slow and clumsy, it hurts my hair.
Not at all like the prince.
He gets here in a minute!"

"Wicked child!" screamed the witch.
"What are you saying?
I hid you away here so no one could find you.
What have you done?
You tricked me! You tricked me!"

The witch was so angry,
she took out her scissors.
And *snip snap!*
She cut off Rapunzel's braids.
The long golden braids
fell to the floor.

Then the witch took Rapunzel far away
to a lonely place in the middle of nowhere.
And she left Rapunzel there,
to live or die.

That very same evening,
the witch took Rapunzel's braids
and tied them to a hook on the tower window.
Then she waited in the tower
for the prince to come.

As soon as it was night,
the prince came and called,
  Rapunzel, Rapunzel!
  Let down your hair!

The braids came down as always.
The prince climbed up quickly.
He couldn't wait to see Rapunzel.

But instead of Rapunzel,
there was the witch!

"Your little songbird is gone,"
the witch said.
"The cat took her away. Too bad!
You will never hear her singing. Never!
She is lost to you forever.
And before the cat is through,
she will scratch your eyes out.
You will never see Rapunzel again!"

When he heard those terrible words,
the prince jumped from the tower.
He landed in a thornbush,
and the thorns scratched his eyes.
From that moment,
the prince was blind.

For years, the prince wandered
in the forest.
Then, one day he came to a lonely place
in the middle of nowhere.

Someone was singing.
The prince stopped to listen.
The singing grew louder and clearer.
Could it be...?
It was!

It was Rapunzel!

Rapunzel knew the prince at once
and ran to meet him.
When she saw he was blind,
she began to cry.
Her tears fell on the prince's eyes.
Suddenly he could see again!

The prince took Rapunzel to his kingdom.
There they were married
and lived happily together
for a long, long time.